D0646515

This book belongs to

_____

The Bunnies'

Trip

by Lezlie Evans

illustrations by Kay Chorao

HYPERION BOOKS FOR CHILDREN
NEW YORK

Text © 2008 Lezlie Evans   Illustrations © 2008 by Kay Sproat Chorao   All rights reserved.
Published by Hyperion Books for Children, an imprint of Disney Book Group.
Printed in Singapore   First Edition   10 9 8 7 6 5 4 3 2 1   Library of Congress Cataloging-in-Publication Data on file.
ISBN-13: 978-0-7868-1898-3   ISBN-10: 0-7868-1898-0   Reinforced binding   Visit www.hyperionbooksforchildren.com

The bunnies eight all celebrate,
for they no longer have to wait.

Vacation time is finally here!
Let's get this bunnies' trip in gear!

Bunnies one and two rush off
to get the suitcase from the loft.

Bunnies three and four help out
by mapping out the travel route.

Bunnies five and six prepare
a tasty spread of road-trip fare.

Bunnies seven and eight's big chore
is mopping up the kitchen floor.

Here comes the case from off the rack.
Every bunny come and pack!

Eight bunnies stuff.
Eight bunnies cram.
And in one suitcase, all eight jam

all sorts of things for bunny travel,
but soon their plan starts to unravel.

Bunnies one and two both say,
"This lid won't shut. There's just no way!"
Bunnies three and four propose,
"Let's put on all the extra clothes!"

Bunnies five and six agree.
They pull on hats, boots, dungarees.
Bunnies seven and eight pile on
four layers till the heap is gone.

The lid now shuts, that much is true,
but such a harebrained plan won't do!

One by one, they all concede
another case is what they need.

Now bunnies one through four will pack,

while bunnies five through eight all stack
their things into the second case.

But once again, they're out of space.

"We are not taking these or those—
Just who put in this garden hose?"

Out come a horn, harebrush, and skates,

Gran's frying pan,

a hat, and weights.

All sorted out, no time to waste,
"Let's get this packing done with haste!"
Hooray! They've lightened up the load.

They're ready now to hit the road.
"Let's grab the food, turn off the lights.
Last one out, please lock up tight!"

As merrily they hop along,

they share some snacks and sing some songs.

They travel well into the night.
Eight worn-out rabbits—what a sight!

"Bunny one is bothering me!"
Bunny two says irritably.
Bunnies three and four insist—
"We'll stop right here if you persist!"

Bunnies five and six can see
the little ones are all weary.

Bunnies seven and eight both drop
"We can't go on, not one more hop."

"Jump on our backs. We'll carry you!
Our lengthy journey's almost through."

Way up ahead, they spy a light.
The bunnies bounce with all their might!

When, finally, the crew hops in
they greet their favorite bunny kin.
Great-aunties here, great-uncles there,
and bunny cousins everywhere!

With hugs for all and happy tears,
it seems as though it has been years
since they have seen this welcome sight!
Their noses nuzzle in delight.

Now that their traveling is done,

it's time to have some bunny fun!

At least, until it's time for them
to pack up and head home again!